MR PLOD'S BOSSY DAY

First published in Great Britain by HarperCollins Publishers Ltd in 1998

1 3 5 7 9 10 8 6 4 2

ISBN: 0 00 136087 6

Cover design and illustrations by County Studio

A CIP catalogue record for this title is available from the British Library.

Printed and bound in Belgium by Proost

Enid Blyton™

TOYLAND STORIES™

MR PLOD'S BOSSY DAY

Collins

An Imprint of HarperCollins*Publishers*

Mr Plod was having just the sort of day he liked. A very bossy day!

First he'd put the goblins in prison for stealing cakes.

Then he told Noddy off for driving too fast.

"I wasn't driving too fast!" Noddy complained. "It just *looked* very fast because you were walking so slowly. It's those flat feet of yours."

This made Mr Plod even more bossy than ever.

"None of that, my lad," he huffed crossly. "You're in enough trouble as it is. Now where's my notebook?"

And with a very important look on his face, he reached for his top pocket.

"DRIVING - TOO - FAST,"

he said loudly as he wrote it all down in his notebook. "That will be a fine of two sixpences," he told Noddy.

"But I don't have two sixpences," Noddy replied. "You'll have to wait until I have picked up some passengers and earned some money."

Mr Plod gave Noddy a very serious frown.

"Hum!" he said gruffly. "Well - as soon as you *have* earned two sixpences, just make sure you bring them straightaway to my police station!"

Feeling very pleased with himself, Mr Plod turned away and marched back towards his police station. He rubbed his hands with glee. Now to give those goblins another good telling-off...

But when Mr Plod entered his police station, he was in for a very nasty shock.

The door to the prison was wide open.

The goblins had ESCAPED!

Mr Plod just couldn't believe it. He was so miserable!

"Ah, that's the problem," he sighed as he took the prison key from his pocket and tried it in the lock. "The lock is broken. The key doesn't fit any more."

He tried jiggling the key about in the lock once more to see if that would help. First he jiggled it to the left and to the right. Then he jiggled it up and down.

But the prison door still came open every time he tugged it.

So Mr Plod stepped inside the prison and put the key in the lock from the other side. He held his breath on hearing a little click inside the lock. Had he done the trick this time?

Yes - he had! He pushed the prison door once more just to check. It stayed closed.

"It just needed a few brains, that's all!" he said to himself with a smile, as he turned the key the other way to open the door again.

But the door wouldn't open. The lock must have jammed again. Mr Plod was locked inside the prison!

"HELP! HELP!" he cried. "Please! Someone come and let me out!"

Sadly, none of the passers-by could hear him. Or if they could hear him, they thought it was only one of the goblins calling out from the prison - and so they just continued on their way!

Getting more and more miserable, Mr Plod watched the minutes slowly tick by on the clock. He was getting fed up. He was getting hungry. He just wished someone would come and let him out!

At last, Mr Plod heard someone approach the door of the police station. He smiled as he saw the door open. It was Noddy.

"I've come to pay you my two sixpences," Noddy said. "I'm sorry it took so long, but -"

Noddy gasped when he realised that Mr Plod wasn't sitting behind his desk but was inside the prison.

"Why, Mr Plod!" he exclaimed. "Whatever are you doing, sitting in there?"

Mr Plod looked so unhappy staring out from behind the bars.

When Mr Plod explained what had happened, Noddy started to chuckle. But then he also felt very sorry for him.

“I’ll just go and fetch Mr Sparks,” Noddy said, hurrying towards the door. “He will get you out.”

It seemed to Mr Plod that Noddy was gone for hours. Hours and hours! But at last, Noddy came back into the police station, accompanied by Mr Sparks and his tool box.

"Tut, tut, tut," said Mr Sparks as he started to poke at the lock with one of his screwdrivers. "A tough job here and no mistake. It could take me ages!"

Poor Mr Plod's face became gloomier than ever. After a while, though, there was a sudden click inside the lock, and the door opened.

Mr Plod was free at last!

He was so happy that he soon started to get bossy again. He tucked his thumbs inside the top of his tunic.

"Now, Noddy," he said in a deep, serious voice. "Where are those two sixpences you were going to pay me because you were driving too fast?"

But Noddy told him that he no longer had the sixpences. He'd given them to Mr Sparks.

"Yes, that's right," said Mr Sparks. "Two sixpences. That's what I always charge for an emergency call out."

Mr Plod started to get very cross. How dare Noddy give Mr Sparks his two sixpences!

But then Mr Plod realised that if Noddy *hadn't* paid Mr Sparks the two sixpences, Mr Sparks wouldn't have come to rescue him.

Slowly, Mr Plod started to smile. Then he began to chuckle out loud.

"I suppose it all serves me right for being too bossy," he laughed.

And he promised he would never be too bossy again. Well, at least... not for the rest of the day!

THE NODDY CLASSIC LIBRARY

by Enid Blyton™

1. NODDY GOES TO TOYLAND
2. HURRAH FOR LITTLE NODDY
3. NODDY AND HIS CAR
4. HERE COMES NODDY AGAIN!
5. WELL DONE NODDY!
6. NODDY GOES TO SCHOOL
7. NODDY AT THE SEASIDE
8. NODDY GETS INTO TROUBLE
9. NODDY AND THE MAGIC RULER
10. YOU FUNNY LITTLE NODDY
11. NODDY MEETS FATHER CHRISTMAS
12. NODDY AND TESSIE BEAR
13. BE BRAVE LITTLE NODDY!
14. NODDY AND THE BUMPY-DOG
15. DO LOOK OUT NODDY!
16. YOU'RE A GOOD FRIEND NODDY!
17. NODDY HAS AN ADVENTURE
18. NODDY GOES TO SEA
19. NODDY AND THE BUNKY
20. CHEER UP LITTLE NODDY!
21. NODDY GOES TO THE FAIR
22. MR PLOD AND LITTLE NODDY
23. NODDY AND THE TOOTLES
24. NODDY AND THE AEROPLANE